5491 EN
Stone Soup

Brown, Marcia
ATOS BL  3.3
Points: 0.5

LG

P9-CCM-179

# STONE SOUP

## AN OLD TALE

### TOLD AND PICTURED BY
## MARCIA BROWN

### ALADDIN BOOKS
Macmillan Publishing Company
New York
Collier Macmillan Publishers • London

**Aladdin Books**
Macmillan Publishing Company
866 Third Avenue, New York, NY 10022
Collier Macmillan Canada, Inc.

First Aladdin Books edition 1986

Printed in the United States of America

A hardcover edition of *Stone Soup* is available from Charles Scribner's Sons,
Macmillan Publishing Company.

11   13   15   17   19   20   18   16   14   12

Library of Congress Cataloging in Publication Data

Brown, Marcia.
  Stone soup.

  Summary: When three hungry soldiers come to a town
where all the food has been hidden, they set out to make
soup of water and stones, and all the town enjoys a
feast.
  [1. Folklore—France]  I. Title.
PZ8.1.B816St  1986     398.2'1'0944  [E]   86-10964
ISBN 0-689-71103-4 (pbk.)

TO MY MOTHER AND FATHER

Three soldiers trudged down a road in a strange coun-
try. They were on their way home from the wars. Besides
being tired, they were hungry. In fact, they had eaten
nothing for two days.

"How I would like a good dinner tonight," said the first.

"And a bed to sleep in," said the second.

"But all that is impossible," said the third. "We must march on."

On they marched. Suddenly, ahead of them they saw the lights of a village.

"Maybe we'll find a bite to eat there," said the first.

"And a loft to sleep in," said the second.

"No harm in asking," said the third.

Now the peasants of that place feared strangers. When they heard that three soldiers were coming down the road, they talked among themselves.

"Here come three soldiers. Soldiers are always hungry.
But we have little enough for ourselves." And they hurried to hide their food.

They pushed sacks of barley under the hay in the lofts.
They lowered buckets of milk down the wells.

They spread old quilts over the carrot bins. They hid their cabbages and potatoes under the beds. They hung their meat in the cellars.

They hid all they had to eat. Then — they waited.

The soldiers stopped first at the house of Paul and Françoise.

"Good evening to you," they said. "Could you spare a bit of food for three hungry soldiers?"

"We have had no food for ourselves for three days," said Paul. Françoise made a sad face. "It has been a poor harvest."

The three soldiers went on to the house of Albert and Louise.

"Could you spare a bit of food? And have you some corner where we could sleep for the night?"

"Oh no," said Albert. "We gave all we could spare to soldiers who came before you."

"Our beds are full," said Louise.

At Vincent and Marie's the answer was the same. It had been a poor harvest and all the grain must be kept for seed.

So it went all through the village. Not a peasant had

any food to give away. They all had good reasons. One
family had used the grain for feed. Another had an old
sick father to care for. All had too many mouths to fill.

The villagers stood in the street and sighed. They looked as hungry as they could.

The three soldiers talked together.

Then the first soldier called out, "Good people!" The peasants drew near.

"We are three hungry soldiers in a strange land. We have asked you for food, and you have no food. Well then, we'll have to make stone soup."

The peasants stared.

Stone soup? That would be something to know about.

"First we'll need a large iron pot," the soldiers said.
The peasants brought the largest pot they could find.
How else to cook enough?

"That's none too large," said the soldiers. "But it will
do. And now, water to fill it and a fire to heat it."

It took many buckets of water to fill the pot. A fire was built on the village square and the pot was set to boil.

"And now, if you please, three round, smooth stones."

Those were easy enough to find.

The peasants' eyes grew round as they watched the soldiers drop the stones into the pot.

"Any soup needs salt and pepper," said the soldiers, as they began to stir.

Children ran to fetch salt and pepper.

"Stones like these generally make good soup. But oh, if there were carrots, it would be much better."

"Why, I think I have a carrot or two," said Françoise,
and off she ran.

She came back with her
apron full of carrots from the
bin beneath the red quilt.

"A good stone soup should have cabbage," said the soldiers as they sliced the carrots into the pot. "But no use asking for what you don't have."

"I think I could find a cabbage somewhere," said
Marie, and she hurried home. Back she came with three
cabbages from the cupboard under the bed.

"If we only had a bit of beef and
a few potatoes, this soup would be
good enough for a rich man's table."

The peasants thought that over. They re-
membered their potatoes and the sides of beef
hanging in the cellars. They ran to fetch them.

A rich man's soup—and all from a few stones. It
seemed like magic!

Ah," sighed the soldiers as they stirred in the beef and potatoes, ve only had a little barley and a cup of milk! This soup would be r the king himself. Indeed he asked for just such a soup when last ined with us."

e peasants looked at each other. The soldiers had entertained the ! Well!

ut—no use asking for what you don't have," the soldiers sighed. e peasants brought their barley from the lofts, they brought their from the wells. The soldiers stirred the barley and milk into the ning broth while the peasants stared.

At last the soup was ready.

"All of you shall taste," the soldiers said. "But first a
table must be set."

Great tables were placed in the square. And all around
were lighted torches.

Such a soup! How good it smelled! Truly fit for a king. But then the peasants asked themselves, "Would not such a soup require bread—and a roast—and cider?" Soon a banquet was spread and everyone sat down to eat.

Never had there been such a feast. Never had the peasants tasted such soup. And fancy, made from stones!

They ate and drank and ate and drank. And after that they danced.

They danced and sang far into the night.

At last they were tired. Then the three soldiers asked,
"Is there not a loft where we could sleep?"

"Let three such wise and splendid gentlemen sleep in a loft? Indeed! They must have the best beds in the village."

So the first soldier slept in the priest's house.

The second soldier slept in the baker's house.

And the third soldier slept in the mayor's house.

In the morning the whole village gathered in the
square to give them a send-off.

"Many thanks for what you have taught us," the peasants

said to the soldiers. "We shall never go hungry, now that we know how to make soup from stones."

"Oh, it's all in knowing how," said the soldiers, and off they went down the road.